Don't
Look
Away
(See Me)
Oshri

# Don't Look Away (See Me)

by Oshri Liron Hakak

BUTTERFLYON BOOKS

Published by Butterflyon Books
Los Angeles
ISBN 978-1-964420-06-6

To my fellow dwellers
in this place
of cracked
concrete.

You are seen
and loved.

I may live on the sidewalk,
maybe just around your block.

When you turn your head
to look away,
it can be enough
to dim my day.

It's not that I want your pity...
it's just a really tough city.

The cracks that I
have fallen through...
I'm glad they didn't
get you, too.

A million things
could have landed me here...
one being that the world
can be very unfair.

And cracks don't stop to ask why
you're falling through them
when they pull you in.

Maybe you don't have food
or money to share...
But even a look is nice,
to show you're aware.

Could you spare to be
a little less too busy?
Because denying me even a glance
can make me kind of dizzy.

Sometimes I'm just hungry
for a twinkle of your care,
Which is different
from your gaping stare.

You know —
the one that eyes me
long in judgment,
but doesn't see me
beyond my predicament.

Doesn't see that
we're like each other...
Doesn't see that I, too,
come from a mother.

That I laugh, too.
That I cry, like you.

That I am someone's child,
sister, brother, auntie,
uncle, friend, too.
That I have memories
of joy and love, like you.

That I have people
I care deeply about, too.
That I have given
of myself to others, like you.

That I have celebrated victories
and mourned missteps, too.
That I have been a vessel
of healing and kindness, like you.

That I have painted pictures
and sung songs, too.
That I'm a human being, like you.

And all I'm saying, fellow dweller,
in this place of cracked concrete...
Please see me like you remember that
as you pass me on the street.

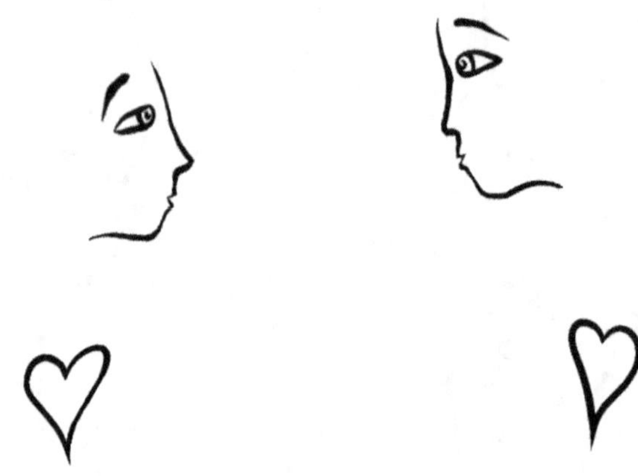

Can we picture an alternate reality,
where our worth is unbound to realty?

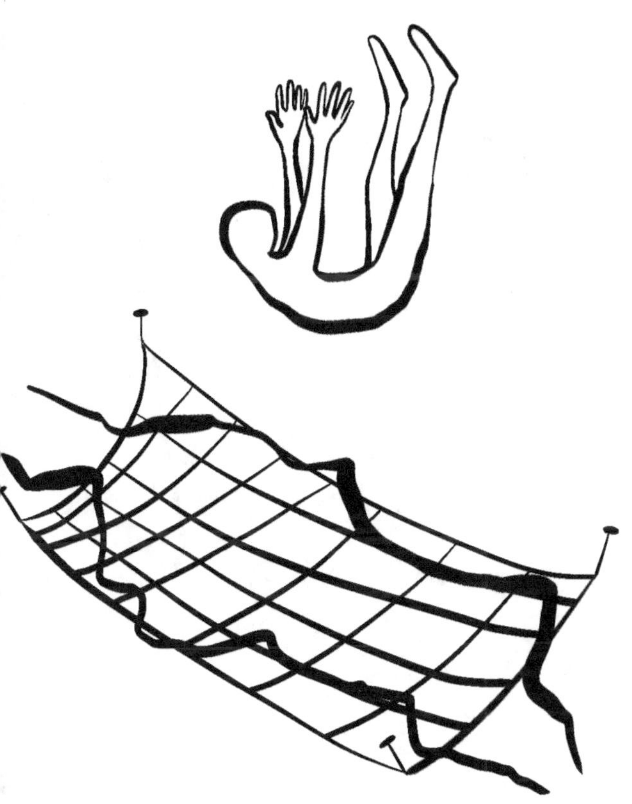

What steps would create a net
that celebrates human worth,
rather than fixating on the fantasy
we have come to call net worth?

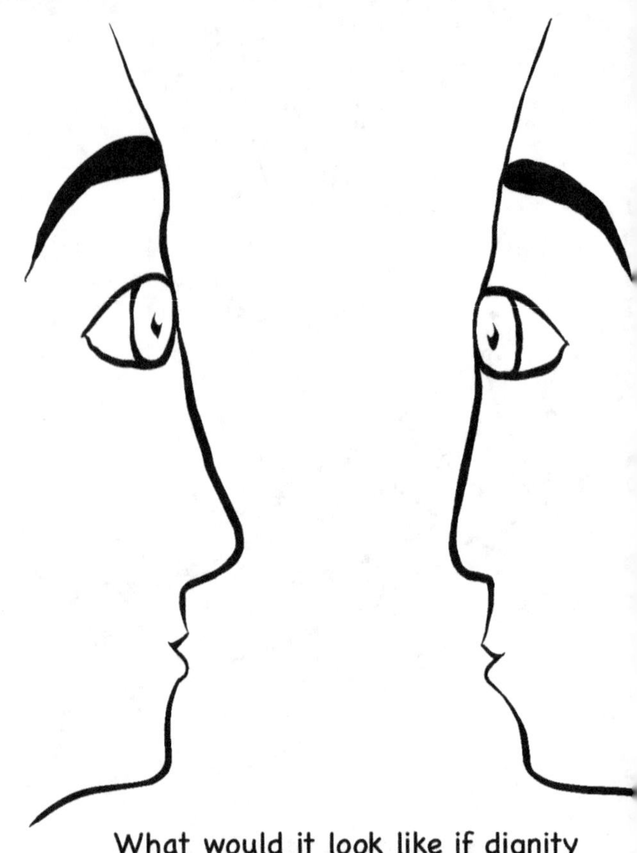

What would it look like if dignity
were not something to buy,
and we made a world where we could
look each other straight in the eye?

# The Mend

# Resources

Mean Streets: Homelessness, Public Space,
and the Limits of Capital
by Don Mitchell
( https://ugapress.org/book/
9780820356907/mean-streets/ )

Los Angeles Poverty Department
and the Skid Row Museum
https://www.lapovertydept.org/

LA Street Care
https://opencollective.com/lastreetcare
@lastreetcare

# Thanks

Big thanks to Hillary Barker for your
huge heart and for helping to inspire this
book. Find mor out more about Hillary
here: hillarybarker.com

More about Oshri here ButterflyonBooks.com
and on IG @oshrihakak

www.ingramcontent.com/pod-product-compliance
Lightning Source LLC
Chambersburg PA
CBHW070216010826
48976CB00014B/2646